and looked after it to help it grow straight and strong

To Nicholas, Rose and Alexander

British Library Cataloguing in Publication Data
Purves, Libby, *1950*–
The hurricane tree
I. Title   II. Lamont, Priscilla
823'.914 [J]
ISBN 0-370-31247-3
Text copyright © Libby Purves 1988
Illustrations copyright © Priscilla Lamont 1988
Printed and bound in Italy for
The Bodley Head Ltd
32 Bedford Square, London WC1B 3EL
by Imago Publishing Ltd
First published 1988

The Hurricane Tree

Libby Purves

Illustrated by Priscilla Lamont

The Bodley Head
London

Once upon a time there was a boy called William, who lived in an old house underneath a tall tree.

In the spring the tree was like a big pale green umbrella, higher than the rooftop, and if William looked up into the branches, he could see birds building their nests.

In the summer, he had his lunch under the tree, then leaned on its smooth warm trunk and fed the crumbs to the squirrels.

In the autumn, the tree dropped sticky prickly beech-nuts into William's sandpit, and threw down heaps of dry golden leaves. He made beds out of them, and mountains, and kicked them into snowstorms.

And in the winter, when the real snow came, his mummy sometimes took him to the kitchen window at bedtime, to see the big yellow moon through the top of the tree. "It looks like a balloon tangled up in the branches," said William. "One day, when I'm big, I'm going to climb right up that tree and sit next to a bird's nest and look at the stars."

"It's a very old tree," said William's daddy. "It's more than a hundred years old. Someone must have planted it in the old days, and looked after it to help it grow straight and strong."

"What was it like in the old days?" said William.

"Well," said his daddy, "I wasn't even born then, so I don't remember. But when that tree was a new shoot, there weren't any cars, or aeroplanes, or tractors. Big brown horses worked on the land instead, pulling ploughs and carts. And the people didn't have electricity, either. They cooked their food on wood fires."

"Just like a barbecue," said William.

"They didn't have electric lights, either," said his mummy. "The children had candles to light them to bed."

But one night, very late, William woke up feeling a bit frightened. A wind was blowing outside, a very strong wind indeed. He could hear the tiles rattling on the roof, and the trees sighing and creaking. The noise made him sad. He climbed out of bed and went to the window, but everything was black outside, because there was no moon. He couldn't see the garden, and he couldn't see the tree. Something went CRASH! in the dark, and his little sister Lucy started to cry in her sleep. William had to keep his eyes shut, so he didn't cry too.

Suddenly his daddy came in with a torch in his hand, making big black shadows on the wall. "The electricity isn't working. I think the wind must have blown the wires down. But we can see all right with the torch. You two can come into bed with Mummy and me."

William tried to sleep in the big bed, but the wind was still howling around the house and whistling in the chimney-pots, and he kept thinking about the birds in the tall tree branches. "Will they be all right in the wind?" he asked. But his mummy and daddy were asleep. Once he thought he heard a cracking sound, and a sigh, out in the garden. Then he went to sleep too.

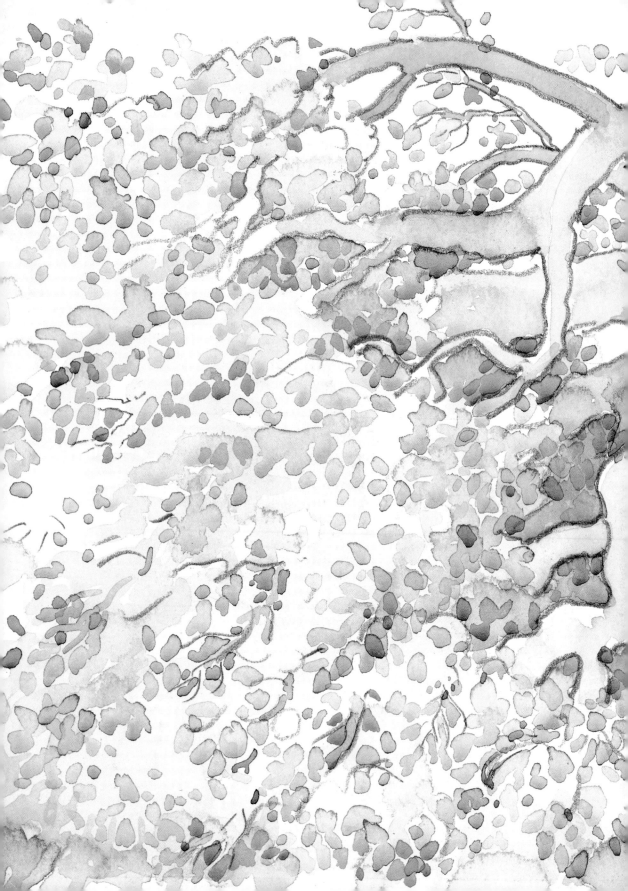

In the morning, the family came downstairs and looked out of the window. "Oh!" they all shouted together. The big beech tree was down. The wind had knocked it right over in the night. You could see its roots tipped up against the sky, and even the very top branches were lying on the ground, in the mud by the garden gate. And all the secret shadows had gone from the garden.

William began to cry. "You said it took a hundred years to grow that tree!" he sobbed. "But people don't live as long as that. I will be dead before it can grow up again so beautiful."

He wouldn't eat his breakfast, and he wouldn't play with his toys. He didn't even care when Lucy borrowed his best clockwork train. Daddy said that William could help to put some tiles back on the roof, but William said, "No. I don't want to do anything. I want my tree to stand up again."

"Well, it can't," said Daddy. He went off to fix the roof, and William just stood and looked at the poor old tree.

"Well, it can't," said Daddy. He went off to fix the roof,
and William just stood and looked at the poor old tree.

After a while William said, "May I climb on it?"

"Yes," said Daddy. And he helped him up. William sat on the trunk and held on to a high branch. "I'm a squirrel," he said. Daddy lifted up Lucy to be another squirrel next to him. "Have a nut," said William kindly, and Lucy ate a pretend nut. Then William climbed further along the tree-trunk, and found a higher branch to sit on. It felt safe and secret, up among the leaves. "The tree is still my friend," he said.

There wasn't any electricity all day, because the wind had knocked down all the poles and wires. "It must have been a hurricane," said Mummy. At lunchtime, they had to make a fire of branches and leaves, and cook sausages on it. "We're cooking on a wood fire," said William. "Just like in the old days when my tree was little." He took his sausages and sat on the big tree-trunk to eat them. "Will we have to have a candle to light us to bed?"

"Yes, I think so," said Mummy. "And a lantern, to eat our supper by."

William and Lucy played on the tree all day long. When it was nearly dark, Mummy lit some candles and lanterns and the children came into the kitchen. William did a painting of the tree, and hung it on the wall. Then he said to his daddy,

"Can we plant another beech tree, just like the old one?"

"Yes," said Daddy. "But it won't be big for years and years."

"I know," said William. "But I'd still like to plant one, please."

Daddy was pleased. "We'll find a good place and plant a young tree. But we'll have to look after it properly while it's little. It can be a present for your children when you grow up, and then in a hundred years, your great-grandchildren can play under the tree with all their friends."

"And climb it?" said William.

"When they're big enough," said Daddy. "Anyway, every year the new tree will get bigger and stronger and more beautiful."

"Will the hundred-years children know it was us who planted it there?" said William.

"Well," said his daddy. "They might guess it was someone who loved trees."

William broke off a little twig and took it up to bed with him.

"Tomorrow we'll start to saw up the tree and tidy it away," said his daddy. "But wood is useful stuff. If we save it carefully, and dry it for a year, we'll be able to make new things out of it, in my workshop."

"A chair for the kitchen," said Mummy.

"And a toy boat," said Lucy.

"And a desk for my work," said Daddy. "What would you like, William?"

William thought for a minute. "I want a rocking-horse. Then I can rock on it and pretend I'm a bird on a high branch, and think about the tree that fell down in the hurricane."

"I'll make you the best rocking-horse in the world," said Daddy.

And he did.

Libby Purves is well known as a journalist and presenter of Radio 4's Midweek programme. She lives in a farmhouse in Suffolk with her husband, Paul Heiney, and their two young children, Nicholas and Rose. On the night of the October 1987 hurricane, they lost a treasured 189-year-old beech tree from their garden and the effect this had on her son, Nicholas, inspired her to write *The Hurricane Tree*. She will be donating her share of the royalties to The Woodland Trust.

Priscilla Lamont, a distinguished children's book illustrator, studied at the Canterbury College of Art. She lives with her architect husband and their young son, Alexander, close to Libby Purves in Suffolk. *The Hurricane Tree* is her first picture book for The Bodley Head.

Someone must have planted it in the old days....